THE SECRET OF THE SANTA BOX

WRITTEN BY
CHRISTOPHER
FENOGLIO

ILLUSTRATED BY
ELENA K.
MAKANSI

tpg
Treehouse Publishing Group | Saint Louis, MO

tpg

Published by Treehouse Publishing Group
© 2017, Text - Christopher Fenoglio
© 2017, Illustrations - Elena Makansi

Treehouse Publishing Group is an imprint of Amphorae Publishing Group
4168 Hartford Street
Saint Louis, MO 63116 St. Louis, MO

For more information on Christopher Fenoglio and *The Secret of The Santa Box*,
visit www.TheSecretOfTheSantaBox.com.

For more information on the art and illustrations of Elena K. Makansi, visit
www.elenamkansi.com

Fonts: Avenir Next and St. Nicholas

Library of Congress Control Number: 2017951774

ISBN: 9780996390163

To Mom and Dad for so many magical Christmases, to Denise for
your insights into poetry, and especially to my lovely wife Linda,
my cocreator in this and all our other wonderful works of life.

In the magic of Christmas, where innocence dwells
Amid ornaments, presents, and sweet sounding bells,
There's a legend revered by the young and the old
With a secret more precious than silver or gold.

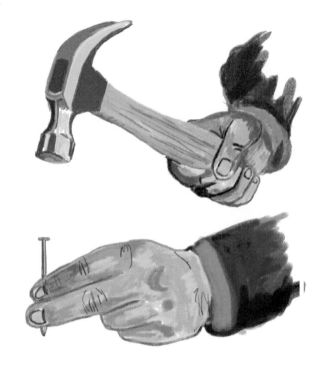

Generations of parents have guarded the truth
So their children can savor the sweetness of youth,
Without worries or burdens of earthly concerns
But with love that creates so much joy in return.

For the young ones will dream about gifts that surprise
Even as they grow older and questions arise.
Homemade cookies and milk they'll continue to leave
As they cling to the facts that are hard to believe.

Like a sleigh pulled by
reindeer that power its flight,

And that Santa Claus visits
each house in one night,

Where he fills all the stockings
of good girls and boys
With delicious confections
and marvelous toys.

There are numerous names for this jolly old elf:
Father Christmas, St. Nicholas, Santa himself.
But the truth about Santa is more than his name.
There's an actual person who's rarely the same.

So to all of you children who search for a clue,
And your parents who wish to give answers to you,
Please consider this tale of a curious girl
Who discovers the truth about love in the world.

When her father brings home a big tree for the den
And her mother hangs stockings and tinsel again,
As the weather turns colder and snowflakes appear,
Little Kristin is certain that Christmas is near.

As she sings about Santa Claus coming to town,
There's a lilt in her voice, a beautiful sound.
She can name all the reindeer, beginning to end,
While she dances with jingle bells clasped in her hand.

'When her mother bakes cookies that sweeten the air,
Helpful Kristin spreads frosting on cupcakes with care.
She's a curious girl and determined to learn
All she can about Santa before his return.

"Can you tell me why Santa Claus wears so much red?
Does he know to watch out for the planes overhead?
Will he take all the cookies we put on his plate?
Does he eat healthy meals? Is he watching his weight?

Do his reindeer get tired? Do they ever get rest?
Should we feed them some apples?
Are carrots the best?
I just don't understand
how he builds all the toys
And delivers them here
without making a noise!"

Glancing up from his book, Father gives her a smile,
Glad to savor this moment of childhood a while.
Because parents can recognize innocence lost
And will try to prevent it, no matter the cost.

Yet he knows that her questions are signs of her growth
And to nourish her knowledge is good for them both.
It's a gift that encourages spreading her wings
And the strongest foundation for all that life brings.

After dinner and dishes, they walk by the stores
to see bright decorations and wreaths on the doors.
All the lampposts are covered with ribbons and bows,
While the lights on the courthouse all glisten and glow.

As they walk hand in hand with their daughter between
They arrive at a church and Nativity scene.
In the stable, the parents and shepherds bow low
To the babe in the manger with the glowing halo.

Just outside of the manger, three kings from afar
Offer frankincense, gold, and sweet myrrh in a jar.
Overhead there's a star that's so shiny and bright
And an angel who heralds the birth of the Light.

At the car lot, three Santas are singing a song,
While two others are gracefully dancing along.
Down the street a short Santa is ringing a bell,
And a tall one has garland and flowers to sell.

APOLLO APOLLO

WHITE CHRISTMAS

MIRACLE ON
34TH STREET

TWO BROTHERS DELI

The department store window displays a red sleigh,
And a Santa who poses for photos all day.
With a white, flowing beard and a red velvet suit,
He sure looks like Kris Kringle, right down to his boots.

When he shouts, "Ho! Ho! Ho!" all the children rejoice
But then Kristin remembers the sound of his voice.
She looks up to her father and says as she blinks
"Is this Santa the plumber who fixes our sink?"

"If this isn't the one who brings toys on my list,
Did the real one retire? Did he ever exist?"
Quite confused and dismayed, Kristin cries in the night,
"There are too many Santas! Oh, something's not right!"

Then her parents communicate only with smiles,
For they know they have treasured this puzzle a while.
They decide then and there that tonight is the night
When they tell her the secret and make it all right.

As they enter their home, before anything's said,
Father turns to his daughter and kisses her head.
With a mixture of wonder, excitement, and dread,
Kristin nervously waits on the edge of their bed.

"With a wink, Father takes from the uppermost shelf
An engraved wooden box that he made by himself.
He declares to his daughter, "It's time that we tell
You the truth about Santa and Christmas as well."

Here's the moment she's longed for, the secret revealed.
It's the truth about Santa no longer concealed.
With a slow, gentle lift, Kristin gazes inside
And discovers a bundle wrapped tightly and tied.

She removes the green string
and then slowly unwraps
A small mirror—"What's this?
Father's error perhaps?"

She examines the glass
But sees only herself.
"What does this have to do
with that jolly old elf?"

"You are Santa, dear daughter, like Mother and me.
There are millions of Santas, as real as can be.
He's alive in our family, our neighbors, our town,
Which is why you see so many Santas around."

"When our Father so lovingly gave us His Son,
'Twas the ultimate gift, a tradition begun.
As we give to each other, we magnify Love
And begin to resemble the Giver above.

We are called to be Santas to spread Christmas joy,
To share gifts with each other and all girls and boys.
What we give can be handmade-just simple and small.
For the Love that we share is the best gift of all."

"Now I see!" Kristin says with her voice full of cheer.
"May I help you be Santa with presents this year?"
"Yes, of course," Father smiles and says with a nod,
"That is how we can share all the goodness of God."

So the next time you question if Santa is real,
Place your hand on your heart and describe what you feel.
For within you, dear children, even as you grow old
Is a Love that's more precious than silver and gold.

About the Author

Christopher Fenoglio has served in numerous editorial, production, and marketing positions in the Christian publishing industry, including *The Tennessee Register, CCM Magazine*, and *The CCM Update*, as well as throughout Nashville's healthcare and country music industries. A graduate of the University of Notre Dame, Fenoglio has recorded three Christian albums, and garnered first place awards by The Catholic Press Association for his writing. He currently serves as managing editor for the denominational website of The United Methodist Church, as well as a cantor and music minister for St. Henry Church in Nashville.

He and his wife Linda have three grown children and one inquisitive granddaughter. They still have the original wooden box and mirror they used to tell their children about Santa Claus and the true meaning of Christmas. THE SECRET OF THE SANTA BOX is his first published children's picture and coloring book.

About the Illustrator

Elena Makansi graduated from Oberlin College where she majored in environmental studies, and is now working on an MFA in Illustration & Design at the University of Arizona. She is part of the K. Makansi trio of writers of THE SEEDS TRILOGY (currently optioned for film by an award-winning independent production company), and is working on her first solo novel. She blogs, runs a Facebook page about vegetables and cooking, and works part-time for an organization promoting farmers markets and local artisans. She has worked on illustrations for several non-fiction titles and has designed many book covers. THE SECRET OF THE SANTA BOX is her first children's picture and coloring book.